Ben and the Big Green Garden

by Alicia Peters

ISBN: 978-1-7781829-0-7

Illustrator: Louise Carota, louisecarota.com
Cover design by: Harv Craven, harvcravendesign.com
Typeset design by Edge of Water Designs, edgeofwater.com

To keep up-to-date with Alicia's writings, check out her website at
aliciaauthor.weeblysite.com
and follow her on

aliciaauthor

Ben is not very **BIG**.

In fact, he's really quite

small.

But even when you're small, you can have *wonderful adventures!*

It is the afternoon, and Ben is chasing his big sister Emma around the yard.

"Stop following me!" she yells. That only makes Ben want to follow her more. Around and around the yard, they go. There is nothing Ben loves more than following his sister around and doing everything she does.

"Go away. I want to play by myself!" Emma yells. She runs faster and faster, and in a blink of an eye, she disappears from sight.

Ben tries to keep up, but he can't.
He runs and falls and runs and falls again.

He looks up, and Emma is nowhere to be found.

"She must be hiding," he thinks. "Is this a new game?" He sees that the gate leading from their yard to another is open.

"Maybe Emma went that way?"

The gate must always stay closed so their dog Penny doesn't get out. Ben is not allowed through the gate, not without mom or dad. They say it is dangerous. Ben feels the little hairs on his arms stand UP. He has never been on the other side by himself, but he wants to find his sister. He carefully steps through the gate.

On the other side is a

BIG green GARDEN.

To Ben, it looks huge, like a jungle. He can barely see the sky. **Green** branches and bushes grow everywhere. Big square stones led him the way his sister must have gone. Looking down, step-by-step, he is careful not to fall in the cracks between the stones.

"Eeeeekk!" he screams.

Something grabs him, and Ben looks up to see **BIG green** leaves and branches. They are reaching out towards him, and there is something with a **BIG red** mouth.

What do you think it could be?

Frightened, Ben falls backward on his bum with an **"*Oof!*"** just out of the grip of the terrible tomato monster. Ben closes his eyes and crawls away as fast as he can. He opens one eye and then the other. Tiny stones are stuck to his hands and knees.

"Ouch," he moans.
Sitting down, he picks the sharp stones out of his skin.

Ben feels alone and wants to go home. "Where is Emma," he cries?
A **BIG** tear falls from his face and splashes on the ground; he notices
a string of busy ants—marching, marching, marching.

Ben wonders where they are going.

"Move it!" one yells and marches right over Ben's leg! Another follows, and then another until Ben has many busy ants marching over him.

Ben stands up, brushing away the ants, and slowly backs away. There isn't enough room on the square stone for him and the ants.

Continuing on the path, he finds some beautiful **purple** flowers. They look like they are floating in the air and smell like his mom's flowery pillow on her bed.

Ben gets closer and notices that what looks like one flower is actually many tiny ones.

He leans closer, closes his eyes, and takes a
biiiiiiiigggg breath in.

BUZZ! BUZZ! BUZZ!

he hears and opens his eyes to see bees coming
towards him!

How many bees were there?

Back on his bum, he goes in surprise!

Up he gets quickly and runs away from the bees.

Smack, right into Emma! They crash and fall.

"Where did you come from?" Emma accuses Ben,

"you're not allowed outside the gate!"

Just as his sister is about to yell for mom,

she sees Ben has been crying.

"Don't cry. Come here, and I'll show you a secret." She takes his hand gently and brings him over to some big bushes. "What do you see?" she points.

Ben looks, but all he can see is a lot of green. Then he notices some purple and white round things.

"Blueberries. Try one." Emma picks one and hands it to him. Ben puts the berry in his mouth. It's hard at first, and then the flavour bursts on his tongue. His eyes **squint**, and his cheeks **pucker**.

"That's a sour one," Emma laughs, "let's find a ripe one. You'll like it better."

Ben is very excited that Emma wants to play with him. He loves playing with him so much he forgets about the sour berry. "Only pick the **dark purple** ones," Emma cautions.

Ben reaches to pick a berry. He **pulls** and **pulls** and **pulls** until the whole bush **shakes**! "Let go! That one's not ready!" Emma says. "Look, here is a ripe one."

Ben stretches out his arm, but he is too short. He can't reach it. He has an idea; he gets down on all fours and crawls under the bushes. It is dark and cool under the bushes. He can see lots of **purple** berries and finds the one Emma pointed to.

Under the cool leaves, he hears his sister scream, *"ahhhhhhh!"* Ben listens.
"Stop. Sit. Come back here."

BARK!

Ben remembers he left the gate open. Penny must have snuck out too! Ben turns
and crawls out the way he has come. He pokes his head out of the bushes,
and a big slimy tongue slurps across his face.

"*Eeewwww,*" he squeaks.

Emma grabs Penny's collar. "Good job Ben. Help me bring her home."
As he tumbles out of the bushes, Ben holds the other side of Penny's collar.
They pull and pull, and Penny pulls back.

Slowly, they make their way
back down the path
to home.

Ben sees the bees, but there aren't as many now.

As they drag Penny past the marching ants, they s^ca^{tt}e^r and run away.

Before Ben can warn his sister about the **BIG green** tomato monster, he realizes that it isn't so scary after all. Back through the gate, they go, safely back from the place that isn't so dangerous after all.

They close the gate, and mom comes out.

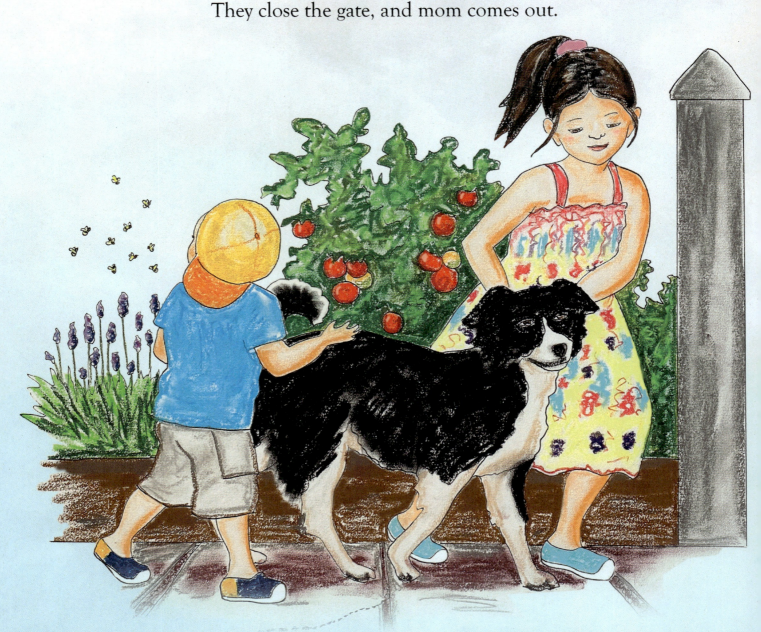

"Leave the dog alone, and don't you dare open that gate. It's time for lunch."
If Ben could talk, he would tell her all about their adventure...

But some *adventures* are only for

little people.